For Katie, Benny and George

with special thanks to
Jessica for inspiring
'the Hummingbird and the Harp'

Brimming with creative inspiration, how-to projects, and useful information to enrich your everyday life, Quarto Knows is a favourite destination for those pursuing their interests and passions. Visit our site and dig deeper with our books into your area of interest: Quarto Creates, Quarto Cooks, Quarto Homes, Quarto Lives, Quarto Drives, Quarto Explores, Quarto Gifts, or Quarto Kids.

Inspiring | Educating | Creating | Entertaining

Text and illustrations © 2020 David Litchfield.

First published in 2020 by Frances Lincoln Children's Books
First published in paperback in 2021 by Frances Lincoln Children's Books,
an imprint of The Quarto Group.
The Old Brewery, 6 Blundell Street, London N7 9BH, United Kingdom.
T (0)20 7700 6700 F (0)20 7700 8066
www.QuartoKnows.com
The right of David Litchfield to be identified as the author of this work has been asserted by him in accordance with the Copyright, Designs and Patents Act, 1988 (United Kingdom).

ISBN 978-0-7112-4725-3

The illustrations were created digitally
Set in Granjon LT
Published and edited by Katie Cotton
Designed by Andrew Watson
Production by Dawn Cameron

Manufactured in Guangdong, China CC112020

1 3 5 7 9 8 6 4 2

The Bear, the Piano, and Little Bear's Concert

David Litchfield

Frances Lincoln
Children's Books

Do you remember the story of the bear
who found a piano in the woods?

It took him on a wonderful journey to the
big city, where he became a huge star.

All of Bear's dreams came true.

But as time went by and Bear got older, things changed.

Bear felt the same, but the pianos became less grand,

The Bear, the Piano, and Little Bear's Concert

the stages got smaller,

and the applause died away.

So, Bear went home.
This time for good.

For a while, Bear found it hard to
fit back into life in the forest.

Sometimes, he missed the city and
the amazing things he did there.

But all that changed when Little Bear came along.

Growing up, Little Bear had so much fun with her dad.
She loved to try new things. Like walking…

rolling in the grass…

swimming in the river…

and listening to the stories of the other bears.

Little Bear never
sat still for long!

Soon, Bear found it hard to
keep up with her.

Especially when she climbed trees,

or chased the birds through the woods.

Then one day, Little Bear found something she'd never seen before.

When Bear caught up, Little Bear asked her dad what the strange thing was. He told her it was a piano.

Gradually, Little Bear learned all about Bear's adventure in the city.

When Bear talked about playing in a band with his friend Hugo, he looked so happy. But there was something Little Bear didn't understand.

"Why don't you play the piano any more, Dad?" she asked. Suddenly, Bear looked sad.

"No one wants to listen to a silly old bear like me," he sighed. "Come on, let's forget all this nonsense and get back to the others."

That night, Little Bear felt so proud of her dad, but she couldn't stop thinking about how unhappy he had seemed.

Looking at one of his old posters, she suddenly had an idea.
She would invite Hugo to the forest to cheer Bear up!

When she had made her letter,
Little Bear asked a bird to take it to the city.

Then, Little Bear waited.
Many days and nights passed.

She started to worry that the message didn't get to
where it was meant to. Or maybe Bear was right.
Maybe no one wanted to listen any more.
Maybe Hugo wasn't coming.

Many weeks later, Little Bear had given up hope.

But then, early one morning, she heard
something coming from deep in the woods.
It was like nothing she had ever heard before.

"What is it?" Little Bear asked her dad as they
followed the sound through the trees.
"It's music," he replied. "Brilliant, beautiful music."

The music got louder and louder as they walked
deeper into the forest.

Then, they saw something that made their paws tingle.

"What are you doing here?" Bear asked, seeing Hugo in the crowd.

When I got Little Bear's message I knew I had to come to t st," Hugo explained. "And everyone else wanted to come

All these animals want to say thank you for inspiring

From all around the world we have: the Tiger and the Guitar,

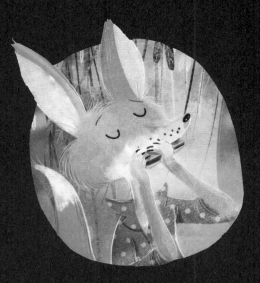

the Fox and the Harmonica,

the Deer and the Kazoo,

the Owl and the Banjo,

the Lion and the Flute,

and the Crocodile and the Harp."

"The one thing missing from our amazing animal orchestra is…

the Bear and the Piano."

As Bear sat in front of the piano,
and touched the familiar keys again,

he realised how much he had missed it.

All the animals agreed that Little Bear's concert was the best the forest had ever seen.

And although it only lasted for one day...

Everyone knew that the music would always stay in their hearts.

THE END

David Litchfield first began drawing when he was very young. His illustration heroes and biggest influences are Albert Uderzo, Sylvain Chomet, Jon Klassen and Shaun Tan. He creates his unique, atmospheric artwork using a variety of traditional techniques, assembling the different elements together in Photoshop to create large-scale, dramatic scenes. *The Bear and the Piano*, David's first picture book, won the Waterstones' Children's Book Prize 2016, Illustrated Book Category, and became an international bestseller.

Also in the series:

The Bear and the Piano

ISBN 978-1-84780-718-2

One day, a young bear stumbles upon something he has never seen before in the forest. As time passes, he teaches himself how to play the strange instrument. The bear goes on an incredible journey to New York, where his piano playing makes him a huge star. He has all the music in the world, but he misses the friends and family he has left behind.

The Bear, the Piano, the Dog and the Fiddle

ISBN 978-1-78603-595-0

Hector and his dog Hugo have made music together through good times, bad times and even some crazy times. But when Hugo learns to play the fiddle, and gets the chance to play with Bear's Big Band, Hector's jealousy gets the better of him. Can Hector swallow his pride and learn to be happy for his friend? This big-hearted sequel teaches that friendship, like good music, lasts forever.